PIRATE TROUBLE
for
WIGGY
AND BOA

Also by Anna Fienberg

PIRATE TROUBLE
for
WIGGY
AND BOA

Anna Fienberg
illustrated by Ann James

A
LITTLE
ARK
BOOK

ALLEN & UNWIN

First published by Dent Australia 1988
First published by Little Ark 1994
This edition published 1996
A Little Ark Book
Allen & Unwin Pty Ltd
9 Atchison Street
St Leonards, NSW 2065
Australia
Phone: (61 2) 9901 4088
Fax: (61 2) 9906 2218
E-mail: 100252.103@compuserve.com

10 9 8 7 6 5 4 3 2

National Library of Australia
Cataloguing-in-Publication entry:
Fienberg, Anna.
   Wiggy and Boa
   Pirate trouble for Wiggy and Boa.
   ISBN 1 86448 253 2.
   I. Title. II. Title: Wiggy and Boa.
   A823.3

Typset in Caslon by P.I.X.E.L. Pty Ltd, Melbourne
Printed in Australia by McPherson's Printing Group
Maryborough, Victoria

Contents

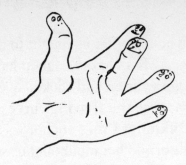

1 That Girl Boa

'Boadicea, you unnatural child! Are you responsible for this outrage?'

Boadicea had been drawing faces on her finger tips with her black and purple pens. When the eyes were just right—crossed and piggy—she pressed her finger tips together and made them kiss in their peculiar squashy fashion. So intent was she on her game under the desk, she almost missed the best part of the morning.

The lesson was supposed to be History, but the teacher had been showing slides of her holiday in Italy. Miss Gizzard had that look she wore whenever she spoke about her Italian Experience. Her eyes had glazed over and her voice became soft as cream as she described the art galleries in Florence and the wonders of a Botticelli painting.

'In the slide coming up, you will see the

Colosseum, where gladiators fought to their death in Ancient Rome.' Miss Gizzard sighed happily.

The projector whirred and clicked over. Appearing on the screen were the flowing curves of a woman dressed in a bikini. A ship's anchor was tattooed on one arm, while across her mountainous stomach were tattooed mermaids with yellow hair, diving amongst sunken galleons. Tiny fish blew bubbles across her navel. She was lounging drowsily against a wall, her eyes half closed, waving a large glass of something dark and dangerous-looking.

From the back of the room came a snort, then a badly repressed giggle, and the whole class rocked with laughter. They whistled and catcalled and nudged each other, falling about in their chairs with delight.

'Who, who, who...' Miss Gizzard bleated. She blinked disbelievingly, stared at the slide, and frowned darkly at the class.

'I saw Boadicea fiddling with something near the projector this morning, Miss Gizzard,' sang out Sam Buzzby. His chest puffed out with satisfaction, and he smiled stickily in Boadicea's direction.

Boadicea and Sam had been enemies ever since Year 2, when Sam had ruined her first—and last—birthday party. He'd sneaked into the dining room when he should have been pinning the tail on the whale, and scoffed the *whole* birthday cake: he'd cheated at all the games, and finally, he'd spilt strawberry milk all over the Persian carpet.

Now Miss Gizzard swung a suspicious glance from Sam to Boa. It was at this moment that she said, 'Boadicea, you unnatural child! Are you responsible for this outrage?'

Boadicea nodded, and stood up. The classroom quietened to an expectant hush.

'Miss Gizzard, you *told* us to bring in pictures of beautiful things. That slide is what my grandfather calls "A Fine Figure of a Woman". Actually, it's my Aunt Gertrude. See, it has written on it, "Caught in a moment of rare relaxation, Xmas '85". I'm sorry if you think Aunt Gertrude is an outrage.'

There was a short silence. The chest of Sam Buzzby deflated, and he looked down at his lap, having found a particularly interesting mark on his shirt.

'I'm sure your aunt is a very good sort of...er—' stammered Miss Gizzard. She had gone very red. But all her training had not been for nothing. She searched for a brisk tone, and found one.

'Well, and now, class, where is your maths homework from yesterday? Exercise books out on the desk, please.'

Ludwig van Weezelman—Wiggy for short—turned round to look at Boadicea. He frowned, Gizzard-like, peering at her over his spectacles. 'You unnatural child,' he whispered, and broke into a laugh that earned him ten extra maths questions.

2 *Bolderack Business*

If Boadicea was an unnatural child, she had good cause to be. What could be more unnatural than living with a retired admiral who treated you as part of his crew? Boa's grandfather had retired ten years ago—reluctantly—after living on ships for countless years. Just how many years, Boadicea could never quite discover.

Once, during a visit to Boa's house, Wiggy van Weezelman had looked at her thoughtfully and asked, 'Exactly how old *is* your grandfather, Boa? Just now he was saying that he'd been mate on one of the first brigantines. Well, he *couldn't* have. That would have been hundreds of years ago.'

Boadicea agreed that the Admiral became very shifty when his age was mentioned; he'd hinted that she would understand when she was a little older.

What Boa *did* know was that he'd captained whole

fleets. He'd steered schooners past whizzing grape-shot and escaped on a raft from a burning ship, drifting for days amongst snapping sharks and poisonous jellyfish. When he was captain of the *Mary Wake,* he'd had queens to dinner, and served French champagne for entrée.

Boadicea understood that this kind of life must be hard to give up. To be reduced to a little house in Seaview Crescent with just one crew member must take some getting used to, after all that excitement and split-second timing. And so Admiral Bolderack, ten years later, still strolled around his yard, swaying to the imaginary swell of the sea and shouting, 'All crew on deck!'—and, if the wind was high, 'Batten the hatches, there's a mighty gale tonight!'

But those nightly promenades were the least of Boa's problems. Admiral Bolderack ran a tight ship. He said so himself every morning, as he twirled his fine moustache and thundered at his crew. Each morning the flag was raised, breakfast eaten, bunks stripped and deck scrubbed, ready for roll-call at 0800. The fact that the crew at Seaview Crescent now consisted of just one member—Boadicea—made no difference to the old sea dog. Discipline and Regular Routine were his favourite things and they could apply to one sailor or twenty. In the

whole of Boadicea's ten years there, she had never seen a day without a hoisting, nor a morning without a roll-call.

Her secret dreams were of mess and laziness. She yearned to lie in bed till noon, eating toast and peanut butter. The crumbs could fall in the sheets and she'd just brush them away idly, as she flicked through the pages of her book and listened to the radio while time floated aimlessly by.

Boa had never known her father. She and her mother had come to live with the Admiral when Boa was tiny, but the itch in her dancing feet became too strong for Mrs Bolderack. She had been a flamenco dancer before Boadicea was born and, one day, shortly after they had moved in with the Admiral, her old partner had phoned from Majorca, offering her a wonderful chance to dance again.

'It will just be for a little while, to see how I go,' she'd said apologetically to the Admiral—and Boa— 'and I'll write.' She kept her promise of letters at least, and they arrived regularly, with parcels, from strange and exotic places. Boa liked to imagine her mother somewhere comfortably tropical, sitting with her feet up and eating breakfast at any old time of the day.

Now, as Boadicea walked home from school, she decided that, all things considered, it had been a satisfactory day. School, with its great possibilities of uproar and chaos, was always a great relief to the Admiral's granddaughter. Today, Sam Buzzby had had the wind taken out of his sails. (Living with an admiral, Boa's language tended to get a bit nautical.) Then, the slide of Aunt Gertrude had livened up Miss Gizzard's 'history lesson'. Boa smiled, kicking loose stones on the pavement as she went.

Soon she came to Wiggy's house, with the tangled garden that looked more like a rainforest than someone's front yard. Boa looked at the weeds with envy. She wished she could be so cheerfully ignored.

As she approached her own house, her spirits sank. She opened the gate, and passed through the neatly clipped hedge. The house beamed at her with its new coat of blue paint, and the weathercock on the roof turned briskly in the breeze.

Admiral Bolderack stood at the door, tapping his watch ominously. 'Three minutes and twenty seconds late,' he bellowed. 'Come on, hurry up now, Boadicea. We'll begin our lesson at once.'

Gloomily, Boadicea followed him down the hall. Inside, she had to blink several times; it was as dark as forty fathoms deep. Although there were plenty of windows, they were all heavily draped with fish nets, studded here and there with the admiral's gold medals. A small fish skeleton still clung to the folds of one window. There could be no doubt that these nets had once felt the swish and swell of the sea.

Admiral Bolderack now advanced into the living room. He took his chair at the table, beckoning Boa to his side. She sat up straight, her knees locked together under the table. The chairs at Seaview Crescent were as rigid as flagpoles, making slouching impossible.

With great excitement the Admiral spread the charts across the table. He circled the islands and cities starring in today's exercise with a sharp red pencil. Little balls of saliva gathered on the ends of his moustache, which he sucked happily. Boa stared moodily into space.

Today, her problem was to navigate a ship from Sri Lanka to the Chatham Islands. She had to calculate the simplest route, including a stop at Bougainville Island to pick up one hundred prisoners and gather supplies. To the east of Fiji, there was to be a powerful storm that would break the mast in two, killing the midshipman and injuring twenty crew. Boadicea had to find a way to repair the mast and double the duties of those remaining. It was not to be an easy lesson.

'Thirty minutes,' announced the Admiral, retiring to the sofa. He rolled forward and back and sideways, lighting his pipe with difficulty. The sofa was filled with water, so that he could never just sit, but rather had to roll with the motion of the waves beneath him. First-time visitors to Seaview Crescent had dreadful problems with that sofa, as tea cups were inclined to spill and stomachs to heave. Not that many visitors came to Seaview these days, as the Admiral regarded friends as an unnecessary interruption to his tight schedule.

Boadicea sat and chewed her pencil. She shifted her weight from one buttock to the other, her spine grating against the hard chair. She stared at the Admiral, who was puffing contentedly at his pipe with his eyes closed, swaying upon some imaginary sea. Boa could hear the voices of other children in the street, playing handball.

She decided she would have to stop—or explode. She dropped her head down on the table and held her breath. This, she had discovered, caused her face to become blue, then white, and the sweat to start on her forehead.

'I'm sorry, Grandfather, but I can't go on. I have this terrible headache. I feel like I've swallowed a bucket of bilge water.'

Admiral Bolderack struggled up from the sofa. He felt her forehead and clicked his tongue.

'Off to bed with you, lassie, you're as white as a blessed seagull. Stay there and I'll call the doctor—he'll know what to do with you.'

'No, no,' protested Boa wildly, 'that is, I don't feel sick exactly, just sort of head-achey, tired—an hour's rest will fix me up, and I'll be as steady as a sail in the wind, you'll see!'

Boa had had experience with the doctor. He was an old friend of the Admiral's, and had sailed with him for thirty years. He was very fond of cutting off legs, was known to diagnose scurvy instead of influenza, and prescribe green tablets that tasted like old nails. Being sick in the Bolderack household was not to be undertaken lightly.

Boadicea crept off to bed. She lay curled under the sheet, pillows bunched behind her head. An

hour passed, and still she lay there, her mind rippling gently over her thoughts like water over pebbles. A sense of peace washed over her. She felt she could have lain there, just so, for ever.

'1700 hours, Boa m'dear, time to fill the belly!' The Admiral's voice crashed into the quiet like guns at dawn. Boa jumped, her heart racing. She stared up at the ceiling all hung about with sails and pennants, and moaned.

'Steady on our pins are we now, Boa?' the Admiral shouted. She could imagine him out there, pacing up and down the passage, dying to get out onto the porch for the lowering of the flag. Dinner could not be touched until the ceremony was completed.

'Aye, aye,' called Boa hastily, thinking of the doctor and his green seaweed medicine. She drew on a cardigan, as these ceremonies in the cold twilight were not brief. Together they marched out into the darkening garden. They stood at attention while 'A Life on the Ocean Waves' played on the gramophone, then they saluted the flag. Pins and needles raced along Boa's arm, until she began pulling at the ropes. The Admiral heaved a sigh like the dying of the wind and it was over for today.

Back in the kitchen, Boa surveyed the shelves with despair. Tinned beans, tinned beef, tinned kidneys and tinned corn stood neatly arranged before her. 'Canned chow, that's the tucker for men at sea,' the Admiral often said. 'No use buying that fresh muck, goes off in the blink of an eye.' The Admiral would not raise an eyebrow at the odd weevil nestling in a packet of flour, either. It made him feel at home.

Sometimes, to prevent death by starvation, Boadicea bought fresh fruit and perhaps a piece of chicken, which she kept hidden behind the bottled water in the fridge. At night she'd steal into the kitchen and devour her meal with the relish which only a week's hunger can bring.

Now she put a dollop of lard into the pan, and poured in the kidneys and beans. She tried to breathe through her mouth as she stirred. Boa sometimes thought how wonderful it would be to sit down to a dinner cooked by someone else. Roast pork, for instance, with apple sauce, and crispy fried potatoes. Then perhaps a chocolate cake, with layers of real cream, and imagine, pieces of dark chocolate hidden like surprises inside. But burning kidneys smell, if possible, worse than raw ones, and now the bitter odour rose up into her nostrils. Quickly she scooped the mess onto two plates and carried them out into the living room.

The Admiral had set the table in splendid style

tonight. It must be the anniversary of some Great
Battle, she thought. There were roses and four can-
dles arranged in the centre of the table, and a glass
of wine for the Admiral. Boa gaped in surprise. Wine
was usually forbidden in the Bolderack household—
it made a crew rowdy and sore heads were no good
at sea.

The Admiral beamed at Boa. 'January the 30th,
m'dear. A day of severe trial and, I might add,
courage. Single-handed I put down that mutiny. It

was led by four ruffians, black-hearted villains with arms like gate posts. Yes, they played a desperate game, they did, and lost. Poor devils,' he added, and smiled slyly into his wine.

'But where did this happen, who were these sailors?' Boadicea couldn't imagine anyone having the nerve to stand up to her grandfather. She felt in awe of those reckless men, standing bold and united against the will of Admiral Bolderack.

'No more questions lassie, there'll be time enough for the whole story later. Let's just pay attention to this good nourishment. Now, what have you got for us tonight?'

The Admiral ate his burnt kidneys with relish. He smacked his lips and burped loudly from time to time while Boadicea ate her beans.

But while she ate, she thought with excitement about the night ahead. The best part of the day was bed-time, when the Admiral came to her room to say good night. Then he would tell her a story about his days at sea: he had fought underwater with the Great White Shark, speared a giant squid, and once, learnt magic from the wicked witch Wyndalena herself. That had been last week's story—while he was prisoner on her island, the Admiral had learned the secret of sailing through Time. He'd then used the witch's own spells to banish her forever from the earth.

Admiral Bolderack became eloquent when he recounted these tales, choosing his words with care as he relived the dangers and daring deeds of his past. He seemed to lose all sense of time; he was no longer the admiral of tight schedules, but an artist of adventure. And tonight, it would be the Mutiny.

3 A Tale of Mutiny

It was still dark when Boadicea awoke. She lay quietly in the grey dawn, and shivered. It had taken her a long time to get to sleep last night. She could still hear her grandfather's words, clearly see the faces of those sailors—desperate, savage, looming… Clutching her pillow, Boadicea had listened unblinking as the Admiral unfolded the tale.

It was a still, moonless night, he told her, as those men had crept along the decks towards his cabin. There were just the four of them: the burly captain and three crew. They were the strongest men on board, and the meanest. As the ship's bell struck midnight they had stormed into his cabin. But the Admiral was ready for them.

Two immediately fell over the rope he'd stretched across the steps leading down to his cabin. He now sprang up, and with just one kick sent the other two sprawling onto their backs. They charged again and again, their knives singing against the air. But the Admiral dodged and kicked and thrust his sword back and forth like lightning, until they dropped their weapons, exhausted.

Boadicea shuddered. She shifted under the sheet, thinking of those four doomed men. The Admiral had devised a punishment equal to their crime. The plank was too easy, too quick. He had banished them, instead, to suffer slowly on a desert island—an island that no one had ever marked on a map. They were still there, waiting offstage from the world, like evil spirits in a play. But they would never, the Admiral had told her, play their parts again.

Boadicea had wanted to know more. 'What are their names?' she had breathed into the dark.

The Admiral had frowned. 'I used Wyndalena's spell to banish those men,' he said. 'Yes, they're safely marooned, all right. But,' he hissed, waggling his finger before her eyes, 'you must never, *never*— do you hear me—never say the names of those men out loud.' Boa had been about to mention that she could hardly say their names when she didn't know them, but she was silenced by his next words. 'For if you say their names out loud,' he'd whispered, 'they will appear.' He had stared deep into her eyes, his finger pressed against her mouth.

Now Boadicea jumped out of bed and switched on the light. She eyed the normal shapes of the wardrobe and the desk and the clothes huddled on the floor, and felt much better. What a ridiculous thing, she said to herself, to think there was any harm in uttering a few names. She flung back the curtains and peered at the slow blossoming of light outside, and the picture of those sailors faded, until it dwindled to a small uneasy speck in her mind.

She climbed back into bed, and nestled into her favourite position; pillow under her head, another cuddled into her stomach. She drifted into a gentle sleep, uncoloured by dreams or sea shapes. From her lips there came a soft burbling, like the purring of a cat.

'0700, FEET ON THE FLOOR!' Admiral Bolderack stood in the doorway, glowing with 'Seafarer's Aftershave' and plans for the day. With his hands on his hips he surveyed the room, clicking his tongue with annoyance. 'Rise and shine, there's work to be done, just look at the state of this cabin!'

The bundle in the bed moaned, and buried itself deeper into the blankets. With two strides the Admiral was at the bedside, his freshly scrubbed face gleaming, his moustache rising neatly at the ends like a ferocious smile. He smoothed one end now, then roared, 'One two three four, feet together on the floor!', and with a flourish he swept the bed-clothes away.

'Ah, what a day!' he exclaimed, marching over to the window. 'There's a brisk breeze blowing, a nor'-easter I'd say, or my name's not Bolderack.' He took a great gulp of air, and thumped his chest. Swinging round to face Boa, he said, 'I'll expect you outside in five minutes—there's the flag to be raised and the deck to be scrubbed this fine morning.' And he clumped out of the room. Boa could hear his enthusiastic footsteps all the way down the hall.

Sighing deeply, her feet fumbled for the slippers lying somewhere on the floor. She pulled up the bed-covers and tucked them in neatly. Then she rummaged through yesterday's clothes and found her blouse. Giving it a quick sniff under the arms, she decided it could stand another wear. She grumbled to herself as she did her chores, and every now and then she kicked a chair, or her school bag, or the leg of her desk. Within six minutes, however, she was ready, and trudged downstairs. The morning ritual had started.

By 0800 the chores had been done, and breakfast remained to be eaten. Boa swallowed a mouthful of cold corn, and hoped that Wiggy would have something decent for lunch today. When the Admiral had finished his meal, he burped with satisfaction and went out to inspect the porch that Boadicea had thoroughly scrubbed.

There was a moment of silence. Then a bellow came hurtling through the air.

'You call this *clean*, my girl? This floor's as clean as the bottom of a sailor's boot! Get that cloth and bucket and we'll try again!'

Boa sighed. She was tired already, at eight in the morning—how would she feel at the end of the day? She saw herself in ten years time, sodden and floppy like a dishrag, her hands dripping with suds, as she bent over that old porch. Her mother had had the right idea. So, for that matter, had those four sailors.

A few doors down the road, Wiggy was patiently waiting. He was immersed in a book, a thin, thoughtful figure with cropped fluffy hair that grew close to his head like fur. Perched on the end of his nose were a pair of steel-rimmed spectacles. Boa was fond of Wiggy, the only one, in her opinion, who was worth listening to at school. He read a lot, and always had something interesting to tell her—like the invention of the new chemical to paralyse sharks or different methods of execution in sixteenth-century

Spain. Boa and Wiggy had both found that in each other's company their houses and families were forgotten. And that was indeed a good way to start the day.

Wiggy leant against the uneven surface of his garden wall. The bricks wobbled here and there like loose teeth, and there were gaps where some had crumbled to dust already. Over the whole grew the wandering arms of the weeds. He kept his back firmly to the garden. Wildernesses worried him.

He was startled, suddenly, by a loud roar. It had to be human, as there were no zoos around that he knew of, and besides, he'd heard that voice before.

Admiral Bolderack was, in Wiggy's opinion, a dreadful man. Whenever he thought of him, the words 'enraged bull' popped into his head. Wiggy had been tossed out of Boa's kitchen several times, with a Bolderack bellow and a box to his ear. Wiggy had since invented a whole series of humiliating scenes for the Admiral. He liked to imagine himself grown tall and towering over him. Sometimes Bolderack was in a Home for Retired Admirals with a bib and high-chair, and Wiggy had to feed him—or not—as he wished. He would explain to the tearful Admiral that only if he ate all those nice fresh vegetables would he get his canned dessert.

Wiggy grinned at the thought, but on hearing a second roar, he decided to hurry along to Boa's house. He arrived in time to see Boa slam the front door with a crash that shook the weathercock on its perch. On her way to the gate she stomped on all the rosebushes. She reached the footpath and swung her bag about balefully. Suddenly, as she glared up the street, the frown disappeared, her lips pursed, and she ducked down behind the hedge.

Wiggy turned to see Amy Parker, one of Sam Buzzby's offsiders, pattering along the footpath. She was humming to herself as she went, dodging the cracks that wiggled across the pavement. 'Oh *no*,' said Wiggy to himself, and he closed his eyes for a moment. He opened them to see Boa leap out from behind the hedge with a howl like wolves after a kill.

Amy yelped as she shot into the air, and she ran like lightning, her schoolbag bumping against her bony shoulder.

Wiggy, from his post at the end of the hedge, wondered for the hundredth time why he liked Boadicea Bolderack.

4   The Subject is 'Myself'

Boadicea was, after all, the sort of person Wiggy usually tried to avoid—dangerous, disorganised and untidy. Wiggy van Weezelman, on the other hand, was an orderly boy. At school, for instance, he always had plenty of space for his elbows on the desk. He kept his exercise books in a neat pile on the left corner, his sharpened pencils arranged in order at the top, and his collection of rubbers (including the one shaped like Ayers Rock that his grandmother had given him) on the right.

Wiggy's workbooks were famous in the staffroom of Stilton Park Public School. At lunchtime, while Miss Gizzard marked her class's books, the other teachers would gather around her and marvel at his perfectly ruled double margins, one in black, one in red. they would sigh over his white pages, untainted by grubby fingerprints or oil spots from greasy chips.

'A *dream*,' Miss Gizzard would gloat over his maths book, 'an absolute dream,' and the others would enviously agree.

Wiggy would in fact have been a perfect pupil if it had not been for his vagueness and his reading. It was not very often that he remembered to listen to his teacher's voice; his eyes were usually focused downward on his knees, on which rested the far more interesting facts of the siege of Troy and Ulysses' adventures there, or, like today, the rising level of carbon monoxide in the world's atmosphere. Of course these subjects left him a lot to think about, and often he would stare blankly into space, causing great irritation to Miss Gizzard and much amusement for those around him.

This first hour in the morning was Wiggy's favourite time. Today, Tuesday, they were doing Composition, and the room was silent, except for the busy scratching of pens on paper. Wiggy liked the quietness; his thoughts flowed cleanly from his head to the paper and the morning sun was streaming gently through the windows, warming the top of his head. Of course, when someone like Boadicea was sitting behind, silence never lasted long. She tended to breathe rather heavily when she got a good idea. She had a bad habit of rocking in her chair and puffing with excitement, exploding now and then with shouts of 'I've got it!' and 'What a story!'

Today Miss Gizzard had set a particularly interesting subject: 'Myself'. 'Describe yourselves,' she had said, 'just as if you were a house or a painting. Pick out the most obvious things you see first, then look at the smaller ones, hiding as it were, in the shadows. See what you can discover about yourselves.' She peered at them earnestly, as if she could see all sorts of interesting things going on in their heads. It is a strange thing, Wiggy thought, that you can live inside your skin for all these years, and yet not *really* be able to see yourself. Now, he could see Boadicea; he could say that she was a funny person who made him laugh, but who also made him nervous. She was rather loud and definitely not relaxing. He liked her long black hair and the little gold earrings that made her look like a pirate. She would do well, in fact, on a ship with a gang of sword swivellers.

As he was imagining this, Wiggy felt a minor earthquake behind him.

'Listen, Wiggy, this is my best yet,' crowed Boa, waving her sheet of paper and preparing to read. The funny thing, thought Wiggy as he picked his pencils up from the floor, was that he was looking forward to hearing her story. Her compositions were always full of adventures, like dreams really, where extraordinary things happened, but were treated as if they were completely normal events.

'Not now, Boadicea,' Miss Gizzard sighed. 'Let the others finish their stories first. Sit quietly in your chair, and don't disturb the rest of the class.'

'Loudmouth,' muttered Sam Buzzby, turning round.

'Slowcoach,' replied Boa, and she poked out her tongue, which had a long black streak where she had licked her leaky biro.

After pondering for some time, Wiggy decided to make a list. He was good at lists—they made his thoughts clear and orderly. He drew a red line down the centre of his page, and on one side he put the things he liked, and on the other, those things he disliked.

Wiggy surveyed his list and felt vaguely uneasy. Looking at it like that, all in black and white, he didn't seem to be a very adventurous boy. Or very interesting either. He couldn't imagine his hero Ulysses liking Scrabble and matching socks. He wasn't sure that he'd like to be a friend of someone like himself. Of course, he couldn't write down all the thoughts that buzzed in his head at night: they

Things I like

- Silence
- Thinking
- Books about monsters and sea adventures
- Tidy rooms with clean sheets
- Matching socks
- Playing Patience
- Scrabble
- My grandmother
- Lists

Things I don't like

- Mess
- Noise
- Week-old washing up
- Untidy rooms
- Mould
- Very loud music (especially cello and violin)
- Parents who don't listen (such as mine and Admiral Bolderack)

Wiggy's list

were too complicated and it would take hours. Anyway, everyone knew that world-famous writers were supposed to be quiet, sitting in their rooms, inventing stories to amaze the world. And that was what he was going to be when he grew up—a world-famous writer. With a final glance at his paper he decided he couldn't add anything more, so he drew a neat red line at the bottom and signed his name in great looping letters underneath. He only hoped Miss Gizzard wouldn't make them read their compositions out loud. Mould, washing up—how embarrassing, but it was the truth, and the Truth was something to which all writers dedicated their lives.

5   The Trouble with Parents

The reason that Wiggy hated mould, washing up and noise was that he had plenty of these at home. His mother played the cello, and his father the violin—*all the time*. Music wasn't just a pleasant hobby, something that was enjoyed on the weekend, like cycling in the park or washing the car. No, Wiggy's parents were Professional Musicians. Music was their *life*, they would often explain, as they hurried off to a Mozart concert or twanged away at rehearsals, Mr van Weezelman in his bow tie, his wife in her long cream gown. Household chores, they maintained, were just a waste of valuable time, and better ignored.

Wiggy, who had eyes and ears for things other than music, had a different opinion. Plates were left in the sink, all crusty with scrambled egg and dried tomato. When the sink got too full, his father would put the ones at the top in the oven, where they could be more easily forgotten.

It was no use talking about Dust in this household, either. Every time Wiggy brought the subject up, his mother just quoted some famous Englishman who had said: 'If you never dust your house, after eight years it doesn't grow any worse.' Once he had enjoyed playing with the dust. It lay thick as icing over glass cabinets and coffee tables, and with his finger, he had drawn lots of pictures—usually of snowmen and toboggans as this went with the white background. But Wiggy had grown tired of the game and developed a wheeze.

When the small brown insects in the kitchen first came to Wiggy's attention, scurrying in between the cake crumbs and the smeared knives, he had not been surprised. But he decided that he'd have to take matters into his own hands. Now, every Wednesday he did the week's washing up. After two hours in hot soapy water his hands wrinkled like an old man's, so he read the ads in magazines, and bought a nice pair of rubber gloves—and some biodegradable detergent. (This was the best kind, the ads said, if you cared about your environment. And Wiggy did.)

In fact, the ads were a great help. They told him

where to buy ready-made dinners in cardboard cartons. And there was such a variety—they came in every nationality. He experimented a bit in the kitchen too, with spicy Indian curries and interesting rice dishes.

If there was one thing he couldn't face, however, it was the bathroom. The shower curtain had once been white, with pink swans gliding over a lake. Yet for as long as Wiggy could remember it had been dark green. Mould, thick and luxuriant, covered the entire surface and gathered blackly in a border at the bottom, with fingers of fungus wandering between the crevices. It was like having a shower in a forest, wondering if some animal was going to leap out of the growth and bite you.

But probably the worst thing of all in the van Weezelman household, was the noise. The mournful notes of Mrs van Weezelman's cello rose and fell, flowing from the living room where she sat in her cream gown, into the kitchen and the bathroom and all the empty spaces in between. Twining merrily around the long sad notes were the dancing tunes of her husband's violin. Locked doors made no difference: in a river of sound the noise streamed in under the doors, through cracks, the tide steadily rising. Wiggy didn't know when his parents slept, because

when he got up in the morning, a concerto had already begun, and he had to use his earmuffs when he climbed into bed at night. In fact, he had taken to wearing his earmuffs most of the time at home. His granny, who understood his problem, had given them to him last Christmas. She had lived with her musical daughter for twenty-seven years, so she knew all about noise and how to deal with it. It wasn't that Mr and Mrs van Weezelman were bad musicians, they were actually extremely talented—it was just that the music never stopped. There was never a pause, and there was nowhere to hide.

The most comfortable place to be in that house was Wiggy's room. It was so clean, with each object so perfectly placed, it seemed that no one had ever actually lived in it. There was no dust, no apple cores or curling sandwiches in this room. With his earmuffs firmly pulled over his ears at night, Wiggy sat in his chair, trying to concentrate on his own thoughts.

On the mantelpiece lay his patience cards, stamp collection and Scrabble board. Often, on Saturday afternoons, he took his Scrabble game to his grandmother's place and he usually won. He knew lots of words because he read so much. He liked that neat arrangement of the words on the page, and the way they carried him into another world. At the moment he was reading *The Manifold and Various Characteristics of Pirates* which was most informative. But his favourite book was *Ulysses*. It was a long and very old story about a man who had a great many adventures at sea, and was always being distracted from his journey home by beautiful women and one-eyed monsters. It had been a great feat to finish such a huge book. When the noise was too great even in his room, he had gone to the park after school to read. It was nice to sit next to a tree in the fading sun, but there was a lot of noise there too, what with all the barking dogs and the little children losing their balls and asking him to please go and fetch them. All he wanted, after all, was a bit of peace to think and read and become the famous writer he was destined to be. But it was not easy.

On Wednesday morning, after making his bed, and flicking a duster over his bookshelves, he went downstairs. There was his mother, frowning over her cello, with sheets of music thrown around the floor at her feet. She had a pencil stuck in the corner of her mouth, and was humming loudly. Every now and then she broke off in the middle of a bar, thought for a bit, then said 'Aha!' or 'No!' or 'Yes, *maybe!*'—and scribbled something on one of the pieces of paper.

'Composing,' Wiggy thought resignedly.

'Mum, listen,' he said standing right next to her ear. 'Our class is going on an excursion next Friday and I need some money and my permission note. Mum? Mum!'

Mrs van Weezelman was staring into space, her head cocked to one side as if she were listening to something that no one else could hear. Wiggy knew it wasn't him.

'Mum, I need that note!' he cried, stamping his foot. His mother wriggled impatiently, and said, 'Ludwig dear, not *now*. I'm right on the edge of a dis-covery, can't you see? I can feel the melody on the edge of my mind, hiding in my toes...it's there, I know it, if only I could reach it. Come back this after-noon, my darling, and I'll play you a masterpiece to bring tears to your eyes.' Lovingly, she stroked the bow across the strings, and smiled.

'OK, I'll just go and chop off my head and bury it in the garden, under all those weeds,' said Wiggy. 'I'm going to the kitchen now to get the dirty meat knife.'

'That's nice, dear,' replied his mother, as she cleared her throat for the next bar.

Wiggy stared at her, at the kitchen bulging with breakfast dishes, and the butter slowly melting in a yellow puddle on the bench. He sighed. It was hopeless. He picked up his school bag and went slowly to the door.

'Have a good day!' *sang* his father in E major, and Wiggy turned to see him emerge from the bedroom, his violin under his chin. His father would be of no use either, Wiggy knew. He had that wild look in his eye and was whirling his bow feverishly. Wiggy slammed the door, and once outside, took a deep, long breath.

As he walked towards Boadicea's house, he thought about Parents. He thought about how unfair it was you couldn't choose them. From birth you were stuck with these people, who were really accidents in your life. He imagined the parents he would choose. They would have nice, normal, dull jobs that finished at five o'clock. They would all eat dinner together, and read in the evenings. They would ask him about his day, and listen with interest when he answered. They would give him excursion notes on time, and the nights would be spent sleeping peacefully.

The more Wiggy thought, the more depressed he became. When Boadicea came flinging out of her gate and saw his face, long and miserable, she knew some drastic action was needed. Immediately.

'Race you, lead legs!' she cried, and punched him

hard on the shoulder. Furious, Wiggy punched back, and began to run. Fury rose in him with every step, fury with his parents, with their noise and neglect, fury with the world, and the wind that whirled against his face and whipped at his legs. Together Wiggy and Boa ran, dodging men with newspapers and dawdling school children. The cold wind dived down into their chests, cutting a sharp pain in their lungs, and when Wiggy arrived at the school gate just a minute before Boa, he was snorting like a savage rhino.

He looked around at Boa, and grinned. She smiled, her chest heaving, and rolled her eyes till the whites showed. Wiggy laughed, and as they walked into school and up the stairs, he realised he felt just fine.

It was just as well that Wiggy was feeling better, as the first thing Miss Gizzard did after recess was collect the excursion money. Luckily Boa had just received two weeks pocket money (with a bonus for scrubbing the deck) and she lent Wiggy his two dollars. While the money was being collected, Boa examined Wiggy's head in front of her. She felt so fond of that thin neck, the two jutting ears and the quiff of hair sticking up from his crown. He always hunched his narrow shoulders like that when he was feeling low. Wiggy was a delicate boy, but he had good ideas, and Boa was convinced that he had a Great Future ahead of him. He just needed someone like her to give him a push.

'Right, everyone. Now hear this.' Miss Gizzard's voice momentarily silenced the class. 'For the next two weeks we are going to study, write about, talk about, draw and act—Pirates! Now, tell me what you think of when you hear the word Pirate.'

Wiggy sat up straight with excitement. But there was a sudden explosion behind him, so that he found it quite impossible to hear all the interesting things the class were saying. Boadicea was crashing about, burrowing in the chaos under her desk, and now triumphantly produced a large book. On its cover there was a fiendish-looking sailor with a patch over the left eye, and a large gold earring in the right ear. Across his chest big red letters spelt the words 'Pirates and Buccaneers'.

Wiggy felt a sharp prod in the middle of his back.

'Look what I brought to school today—I must be *psychic*,' Boa hissed, and held out her book.

'Now, I wonder,' Miss Gizzard was asking, 'who can tell me another word for pirate? Very good, Boadicea. Yes, bucc-an-eer, quite right. Now pirates are known for their violence and cruelty. Does anyone know how pirates punished each other when they misbehaved?

Ludwig? Do you know?'

Wiggy became pink in the face and nodded. But he was not quick enough.

'Oh Miss Gizzard, Miss Gizzard!' Sam Buzzby was shouting and waving his arm in the air. 'They have to walk the *plank!*'

'Yes, that's right,' said Miss Gizzard, wishing that she had a plank for that child Sam (their classroom being on the second floor this year). 'But don't call out again, please Sam. Does anyone know another kind of punishment?'

Boadicea was turning the pages of her book with the big red letters. Now she beamed, and smugly surveyed the class. 'They get put on a desert island, they get MAROONED!' she cried triumphantly. Miss Gizzard nodded, and thought that after the plank, a desert island would be the best thing for certain people. The class began to air their sea knowledge with great enthusiasm, led into perilous but interesting channels by Boa, who had heard of enough sea battles and scoundrelly sailors to fill an encyclopedia.

Mercifully, then, the bell rang for lunch, and the twenty children began getting up and inspecting what kind of sandwiches they had in their bags today.

'Before you go, children!' called Miss Gizzard, 'See what you can find in the library at lunch time, and tell me this afternoon.'

'Well, there'll be at least one or two who'll do it, I suppose,' she said to herself as she made her way towards the staff room and a strong cup of coffee.

6 The Pirates are Coming

Wiggy and Boadicea sat on a wooden bench in the playground. On Boa's lap rested the big book. It was beautifully bound, with a gold border of tiny leaves and flowers engraved into the leather.

Wiggy eyed it with admiration. 'Where did you get it, Boa? It's a treasure.'

Boadicea shifted uneasily on her seat, and shrugged. She remembered how she'd gone looking for a pencil in her grandfather's drawer and seen the key. Dully glowing and old, it had lain heavy in her hand. She'd taken it, and, as she'd known it would, it had opened the rosewood cabinet of Precious Things. There the Admiral kept all his secret documents and special trophies. Of course, the first thing she'd seen was the big book, and she'd just had to have a peek inside. But it was too dangerous at home, with the Admiral perhaps coming in at any moment, so she'd smuggled it out to school. She just hoped she could get it back in time before he noticed that it was missing—otherwise there'd be planks from the roof *and* deserted islands for her.

'It's my grandfather's book,' was all that Boa said. She began to turn the pages, slowly, because the paper was that shiny, expensive kind, and it felt slippery and interesting between her fingers. There were pictures of boats with huge sails, and the figureheads on their bows were carved into leering skull-heads, or had faces with gigantic flaring nostrils and thick lips. 'Ferocious figureheads,' said the book, 'were well-known weapons used by pirates.'

Boadicea twanged with excitement, which dimmed as she looked up and saw Sam Buzzby coming towards her with Amy Parker and other members of his fan club. They found seats further along the bench. As they opened their lunches, all eyes were, as usual, on Sam's box.

'Ooh, Sam, can I have some of that, it smells *wonderful!*' The fans' voices wafted up toward Boa and Wiggy, accompanied by the smell of hot chocolate steaming from Sam's mother's thermos. Sam was famous for his magnificent lunchboxes. His mother was a chef, who found time to make him exquisite little cakes with orange icing and sandwiches from home-baked bread.

'Mmmm, this is excellent cake,' Amy loudly exclaimed.

'It's called a flan,' explained Sam loudly. 'See, it has a thin layer of pastry on the bottom, all crispy and golden, then inside is the creamy custard, and on top these juicy apricots and pears. Just a minute, there should be a little box with some cream in it. Ah, yes, here it is!' And he began smacking his lips and smearing dollops of cream all over the top.

Boadicea glanced up at the generous slices of flan, but before she could manage to look away, Sam caught her eye. He smiled sweetly and said, 'Terribly sorry, Boa, but there's just not enough to go round, see.'

Boa scowled and turned her back, the wonderful book for the moment forgotten. Her stomach was growling with hunger, and all she had were smelly sardines on two stale crackers. Wiggy brought out his lunch, which he'd hastily grabbed that morning and they both sighed at the sight of it. Square slices of smelly cheese that tasted like damp Wettex, inside soggy Saos. The two peaches that he'd thought were such a good idea had squashed in the paper bag.

Wiggy finished first, and after carefully wiping his fingers with his handkerchief, eagerly picked up the book again. Sam glimpsed the brilliant pictures and slid along the bench. He leaned forward, trying to see over Boa's shoulder.

'What's that then?' he asked casually, and yawned.

'Something secret that only Wiggy and I can look at,' Boa replied mysteriously, and she tilted the book so that Sam couldn't see inside.

'Oh Wiggy, look at that,' she cried, pointing at a page. 'They must be diamonds. Look how they glow.' Boa made loud noises of fascination. 'You can get very rich being a pirate,' she concluded, and turned the next page.

Sam hovered around, hopping on one foot, then grunted in disgust and signalled to his fans to follow him. Reluctantly they trundled after him. 'We can get better books than that from the library,' Sam sneered.

Wiggy hadn't heard a word. Totally absorbed, he turned the pages until he came to the centre. Staring up at him was the ugliest face he'd ever seen. It was grinning, with its lips peeled back like a wound, and all its teeth were missing except two at the side. Like fangs they dipped down, long and pointed, over the bottom lip. Black greasy curls hung limply round the face. 'Known by the name of Tiger,' Wiggy read aloud, 'this pirate was notorious for his ferocity.' Quickly, Wiggy turned the next page and there was a man with a low forehead like a gorilla, and no chin. Hair covered his cheeks and neck, gathering in a torrent at his chest. 'Thick Mick,' Wiggy read gleefully.

'Geez, he *looks* thick,' cried Wiggy, nudging Boadicea, who had moved on to the sardines. 'Bet he wouldn't know how to sail a paper boat.' On the next page was a pirate with an enormous belly. His shirt was open to the waist and black hairs curled like spiders on his chest. Rolls of fat hung thickly over his pants. 'G.C. Dan' was the caption underneath.

'Garbage Can Dan, eh Boa? What do you think?'

Boa licked her fingers and wiped them on her

Known by the name of Tiger this pirate was notorious for his ferocity.

legs. 'Gee,' she said, 'what funny names. Tiger, Thick Mick and G.C. Dan. Imagine calling them out at roll call! Here, let's have a look.'

Wiggy turned back to the first mean face and shivered. Boa stared, and a cold feeling like slivers of ice broke out along her spine.

'Tiger!' Wiggy whispered happily. 'Ugh! Look at those teeth.' Hastily, he flicked over the pages. 'But who's this fourth one, look at *this* ugly brute—the Captain—'

'Shut up, shut up Wiggy!' screamed Boadicea and slammed the book shut. She stood up, and shook herself, but the cold sweaty feeling was growing and her uniform was damp against her back.

'What is it, Boa, you've gone all white!' said Wiggy looking up at her.

'Don't know, but those faces remind me of something...something my grandfather said. We shouldn't have said those names, we shouldn't have! Wiggy, I don't know what's happening, I'm scared. I feel sick,' and Boa hung her head, closing her eyes.

The bell rang out across the playground and children began strolling back towards the classrooms. Wiggy picked up the book and took Boa's arm. He felt her tremble.

'Maybe it was those sardines,' said Wiggy. 'They

didn't smell too hot from where I was sitting.'

Boadicea said nothing. She let herself be led back to the classroom.

'All right, class, now I hope you've all been to the library and found some interesting facts for me,' Miss Gizzard said brightly, restored by five cups of black coffee and a good chat.

A heavy silence followed. Miss Gizzard's smile sank into the quiet like a stone into the sea.

'Oh, Miss Gizzard,' cried Sam Buzzby. 'I tried to get a book but Boadicea had taken the best one, and she wouldn't let me even look at it!'

'Thank you Sam, but next time don't call out. I'm sure there were other good books in the library on our subject, if you'd just searched hard enough. Well, Boadicea, why were you being so selfish? Surely you know that the library's books are for everyone?'

Silence. How odd, thought Miss Gizzard, for Boadicea not to have an ingenious excuse. She just sat with her head bowed over her desk. She didn't move.

'It wasn't a book from the library,' Wiggy burst out, 'it was her grandfather's. And anyway, Boadicea's sick.'

'Probably had too much lunch,' smirked Sam and giggled into his hand.

'That will do,' snapped Miss Gizzard. 'Now, come along Boa, tell us what you've discovered.'

Boa looked up from her desk. She was pale and a smear of sweat lay on her top lip. Her eyes were huge and her face seemed strangely thinner, and afraid.

'Good heavens child, you don't look well at all. Whatever's the matter with you?' Boadicea continued to stare straight ahead and Miss Gizzard's eyes narrowed.

'If this is one of your silly games, Boadicea, I'll get to the bottom of it.'

Boa's throat was so dry it was hard to speak. 'I think I need to go home, Miss Gizzard,' she managed. 'I don't feel very well.'

Miss Gizzard studied her for a moment. 'All right, Boadicea. You may go. Can you get home by yourself?'

'Yes. Thank you.' She picked up her schoolbag.

'I think I should take her home, Miss Gizzard,' said Wiggy. He stood up, ready to go.

'No, Ludwig, Boadicea is quite capable of managing by herself, thank you. Please sit down. Now, I have made copies of a sea story that I want you all to read carefully…'

Boadicea smiled weakly at Wiggy and walked out

of the class. Once outside, she started to run. She didn't know what this strange feeling was, but she knew she had to get home. Something was waiting for her there, something she dreaded, and somehow it was all her fault.

Panic rose in her, driving her legs like pistons. Within minutes she arrived at her gate, and she slowed her pace. She walked up the path, hesitating at the door.

The hall was dim as she crept inside, and she had to blink several times before her eyes became accustomed to the gloom. Then she saw something that made her gasp.

Admiral Bolderack was crouched at the entrance of the living room, his knees pushed up against his chest. He was sitting like that because he was tied up with very thick rope that wound from his neck down to his ankles. When he saw Boadicea, he gestured wildly with his head, nodding in the direction of the living room.

Slowly, Boa crept up the hall. She reached her grandfather, then stopped. Peering around the corner, she saw what she had been dreading. Grouped at the side of the room were three massive men, looking dangerously like escaped pirates.

'Ahrr, lads, look what we have here then, the

Admiral's cub!' The ugliest one in the middle stepped forward. He brought his face down level with Boadicea's. He was so close that she could see the pores in his skin, big and grimy and black, especially around his nose. Stuck into the belt at his hip was a long sheathed sword. The man was grinning at her, but his eyes stayed cold and steely, and he bared his two yellow teeth.

'Tiger's the name, ma'am,' he drawled. 'I believe you summoned us. A little late p'raps, but all good things come to those 'oo wait.' He jerked his head at the Admiral. 'Don't you agree, Boldy?' Tiger grabbed Boa's hand as if to shake it, but he squeezed it instead until she heard her knuckles crack.

Boa fell into the room and surveyed the three men. One was lounging in the Admiral's armchair, scratching his belly under a sweaty singlet. The singlet didn't reach his pants as his belly swelled out like a hairy melon.

'G.C. Dan, I presume,' said Boadicea, glad to find her voice steady.

'That's it, girlie. Garbage Can Dan at your service,' and he started to pick his teeth. Whatever he found in there, he flicked onto the carpet, making great sucking sounds as his tongue worked around in his mouth. The Admiral, observing from his corner, rolled his eyes with disgust.

The third man was lolling on the sofa, his feet resting on a pile of cushions. A gold ring encircled his big left toe which he waggled at Boadicea in greeting. Above the spectacle of his feet lay the greater miracle of his body. He wore no shirt, so that the full wonder of his hairiness was revealed. Like a carpet, hair grew from his cheekbones down to his navel and great tufts sprouted from his armpits. He had almost no forehead, so that his hairline practically sat on his eyebrows.

'And you're Thick Mick?' asked Boa politely, wondering how it would feel to have a name like that. He obviously didn't mind it too much, as he smiled quite cheerfully at Boa, rather like a big hairy baby.

'Yes, and you're a fine little girl. I haven't seen one of you for years. We've been away for ages and ages, y'know, and it was pretty lonely, I can tell you—'

'That's enough, cut the cackle,' growled Tiger. 'We're not here on a bloomin' picnic, peabrain.' He turned to Boadicea. 'But now we *are* here, me lovely, we're going to do what we've been thinking and planning and wanting to do for thirty-five years.' He glared across at the Admiral, and his eyes were like two black points of hate. 'Revenge, see? That's wot

we want. ''Ow do yer think yer grandfather'd like a lonely desert island? And you, for that matter, eh?' And his laugh hissed through his two long yellow teeth.

Boadicea's legs started to shake. Time, that's what she needed, a bit of time to think.

'Well, in the meantime, men,' she said in what she hoped was a brisk tone, 'How would you like a nice cup of tea? You must have come a long way, and tying up admirals is thirsty work.'

'Aye aye, a nice cup of tea to warm me poor ole insides,' agreed G.C. Dan, and rubbed his hands together. 'And what about a little something to go with it?'

'Coming up,' said Boadicea and went into the kitchen. She stood at the sink, trying to stop the trembling in her hands. She filled the kettle, then opened and shut cupboards, making busy noises with plates and cups. But she was thinking. How could she make her escape from this house? Not through the living room—she'd have to be quick as lightning. The only other room that led off the kitchen was the Admiral's and that had no door to the outside. But it did have a chimney…That was it! Awfully risky, but what else could she do? She'd seen movies about olden-day chimney sweepers—

small boys who went up chimneys to clean out the soot. They always looked thin and stunted, with hacking coughs. Still, she told herself, a champion tree climber should be able to mange *one* chimney.

Stealthily, Boa tip-toed across the kitchen and into the hall. She turned the knob of the Admiral's door. The hinge creaked. She stopped and held her breath. Loud voices droned on from the living room. With a quick flick of her wrist she opened the door and stepped inside.

Now that she was facing the chimney, it didn't look so easy. It was very tall and narrow. For a moment she envied those chimney sweepers who had tools and a push-up and years of experience. She had none of those things, and no time to waste, either.

She grabbed the chair at the far side of the room and placed it under the chimney. Then she climbed onto it and peered up into the darkness. It seemed to go on forever, just a long, black, filthy tunnel. But wait, there was a brick jutting out above her head. She looked up further. Yes, there was another on the opposite side. And another again.

Grabbing a brick on either side of her, she hauled herself up. She felt for the next, and found it. Now the surface of the chimney grew more uneven, and it was easier to find a hold. But her arms were screaming with the effort of supporting her whole weight. She felt with her foot for the jutting brick and found it. Yes, that was better. Black dust was settling on her head, filling her nose. Then something smooth and alive wriggled against her arm.

'No!' she cried and her whole body gave such a shudder that her left hand went swinging down, losing its grip. The rat scuttled past her and disappeared into a hole in the wall.

Boa clung onto the brick with her right hand. Her legs dangled down into the darkness. Sobbing with fear, her fingers sought a crevice or bump in the wall. She found a hold. As she hauled herself up again, her head swung back and she saw a tiny blaze of blue sky.

She gave a gasp of joy. But in the empty room below she heard something move. There was a clatter and muffled swearing. With every muscle she strained herself upwards; the blue patch was growing, in another few seconds...

Something like iron wrapped itself around her ankle. It clung there, and a voice shouted, 'Got yer!' The hand started to pull at her leg, and she felt herself slipping. She clutched at the bricks as she went down, and then suddenly she was on the ground, her face hard against a muscled chest.

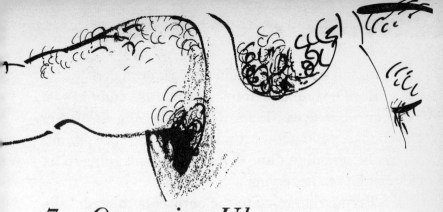

7 Operation Ulysses

Boadicea shook herself free and stared up into Tiger's grinning face.

'Yer as tricky as yer gran'dad, aye, there's no doubt about it,' he growled. His grin withered on his lips as he took her chin in his hand. In a low menacing voice he said, 'But don't try any of yer shenanigans again, small fry, or you'll be drinking sea water instead of yer tea, an' that's a promise,' and he fondled the silver handle of his sword in a meaningful way.

Tiger grasped Boa by the ear and led her back to the rest of the gang. The Admiral twisted and wriggled under his tight rope, but he was as helpless as a caterpillar on its back.

'Found the perisher halfway up the chimney,' crowed Tiger, settling himself at the table. The other two stared at Boa and their laughter boomed around the room. 'She's as black as Mick's beard,' cried G.C.

Dan, and snorted. 'Wouldn't have known her!'

Boadicea rubbed at her face angrily, and the soot stung her eyes. Tears were streaming down her cheeks, yet whether it was from dirt or disappointment, she didn't know. But she wasn't going to let that lot see her crying.

'Permission to go to the bathroom to wash,' she mumbled.

Tiger guffawed and said, 'All right, minx, but mind you don't slip down the plug 'ole.' G.C. Dan, who was drinking tea and eating biscuits at the same time, choked and spat out a mouthful onto the carpet. He enjoyed a good laugh almost as much as his food.

'I'd better go with 'er, there's no telling what she'll do with them windows,' said Dan, hauling himself up from his chair.

He trailed after her into the hall, but stopped at the door of the bathroom.

'Errh, I'll just wait here,' he said. 'Now don't let this belly of mine fool yer; if you try anything funny, I'll be after yer as quick as the wind, see.' And he sat down with his back to the wall, and picked his teeth.

Boa turned on the bath taps. She pulled back the nets hanging across the window and stared out. Strange how that world out there was still going on, people doing normal things like buying tonight's

dinner, walking home form school, playing in the street. Now all those things seemed like a peaceful dream, and this was the frightening reality.

Suddenly a face appeared on the other side of the glass. Its mouth was moving and a pair of spectacles were hanging off one ear. Wiggy! He was pointing toward the living room, mouthing something like 'I saw!' or '*Cor!*' and shaking his head. Boa began to wave her hands frantically and she whispered the word *Help!* Just then G.C. Dan stood up and his mountainous belly filled the doorway. Somewhat embarrassed, he kept his eyes down on the ground, and traced a circle with his toe. 'Errm, you still there, girlie? Watch you don't rub yer skin off, eh?'

'Oh aye, G.C., I'm nearly finished,' Boa replied hastily, and the pirate went back to sitting comfortably against the wall.

Boadicea turned to Wiggy. His eyes had grown enormous, and his mouth was working like a loose spring. *Pirates!* He was saying, *yikes, G.C. Dan!* and other things that Boa couldn't understand, and were not, in her opinion, necessary. What was he doing hanging around, with his nose pressed against the glass? There was no time for games! *Help me!* screamed Boa silently, and flicked her hand in a gesture for him to be off.

Wiggy nodded violently to show her he understood. She saw him clench his jaw with determination, shaking his fist at the window. Boa didn't have a lot of faith, as she turned and regarded the biceps of the pirate guarding the door, but she know he would try anything to help her.

Wiggy raced along the footpath, steaming under his collar with panic. Geez; real live pirates. Had he been dreaming? In his mind he saw again those two men in the living room, the furry one, and the other with his great back to the window. But the worst was that close-up view of that giant who was keeping Boa trapped in the bathroom: the belly, the massive muscles in his chest, the sword at the hip. He licked his lips in fear. He could see cutlasses raised to his throat while he pleaded for mercy; their heartless laughing as they sat around and drank rum over his poor bleeding body.

Wiggy gave himself a shake. 'Get a hold of your-self, Ludwig,' he said. He stopped to lean against someone's fence and delved into his bag. He brought out Boa's book. Gingerly he opened it and saw the face that had so recently been in Boa's bath-room. No other than G.C. Dan. The furry one must have been Thick Mick, and the other...he didn't want to look. He didn't linger over the next member of the gang either: the Captain. He was just glad that he'd stayed on his page nameless and invisible.

'Now Ludwig,' he addressed himself, '*think*. What have you read about pirates? What do you know about their habits, their likes and dislikes, their weaknesses?' He'd only reached the tenth page of *The Manifold and Various Characteristics of Pirates*. And maps and mapping weren't much use right now!

When he arrived home he marched straight up to his room and stuck on his earmuffs. Boa's book didn't seem to go into great details about the habits of pirates: it concentrated on their throat-cutting ac-tivities and the colourful way they swore. He picked up his own book instead, and began to read.

The characteristics of pirates were certainly var-ious, not to say manifold. There were some very long words in all the important places, and he had to use his dictionary every second line. He kept thinking of Boa in the bathroom and the way her mouth had said *Help me!* He felt both terribly important and terribly useless at the same time. Downstairs, the grandfather clock boomed—half an hour had passed already!

Desperately he turned to the third chapter. It was called 'Sea Shanties'. Geez, thought Wiggy, who feels like singing at a time like this? Then he felt something open up in his mind. It was growing, expanding, until an idea, totally formed with a beginning, a middle and an end, emerged. 'I've got it!' he cried and leapt up from his chair.

Feverishly he searched for his favourite book, *Ulysses*. He found the chapter he wanted and began to read. 'Ulysses was sailing home from the long siege of Troy, triumphant. Yet unknown dangers still lay before him—monsters, giants and whirlpools. Circe, a beautiful enchantress, warned him that he would have to pass the Sirens—and that meant certain death. The Sirens were sea nymphs who lived on a rocky island. They had voices like liquid gold, singing songs so beautiful and haunting that every sailor who heard them plunged into the waves, just to stay close to their music.

'Ulysses ordered his sailors to stop up their ears with wax, so that they could not hear the singing of the Sirens. But so curious was he to hear these famous songs that he left his own ears uncovered. Instead, he told his crew to tie him to the mast, so tightly that he could not break free. "Even if I beg you, don't release me," he warned them.

'And so, in this way, the ship of Ulysses passed by that treacherous island, unharmed. The sailors heard nothing, but Ulysses writhed and struggled under his ropes, in an agony of yearning. He became one of the few men to hear the Sirens' song, and live. But as he said later, he would gladly have given up his life to hear those voices for just a little longer.'

Wiggy was thinking quickly. If such a strong sailor as Ulysses was overcome by beautiful music, surely those pirates could not resist? He turned to his other book and found the chapter on 'Sea Shanties'. Further down the page he found the confirmation he needed:

'Pirates,' it said, 'are generally found to be fond of music; in particular songs about the sea. They pass many long dark hours in this way, singing about their loves back home, the loneliness of the great ocean, the ships they have plundered. Sometimes their songs are exceedingly poetic, and they become quite moved. Indeed, the famous buccaneer, Henry Morgan, is said to have rewarded the composer of

"A Pirate's Life for Me" with a large sack of gold.'

Wiggy shut the book with a bang. He couldn't imagine G.C. Dan being moved by anything but a hearty meal. Still, it was worth a try at least!

Taking two steps at a time, he bounded downstairs. His mother was sitting at her cello. She looked splendid, dressed today in her gown of midnight blue. Her eyes were blazing as her bow moved back and forth across the strings, her pearls flashing against the dark velvet at her throat.

'Mum, Mum!' Wiggy shouted, standing in front of her.

'Oh, Wiggy dear, are you listening to my concerto? It's the best thing I've ever done—'

'*Mother!*' screamed Wiggy. He grabbed her hand and took the bow from between her fingers. She looked up at him with a startled blink.

'Listen to me. For *once*,' Wiggy said in the most serious tone he'd ever used. His father wandered over to stand behind his mother. His violin was still perched under his chin, but he had ceased playing. With one hand on his wife's shoulder, he gazed curiously at Wiggy.

'A friend of mine is in desperate trouble. She is being kept prisoner in her house by four savage men—'

'Good heavens, Ludwig, why not call the police, the fire brigade, or one of those trouble-shooting squads,' said Mrs van Weezelman. 'What a dreadful business!'

Impatiently, Wiggy shook his head. 'You don't understand, they're too powerful—they're *magical*, there's no knowing what they'd do to Boa or her grandfather if they saw a whole troop of men standing at the door. No, there's only one thing that could work.' He paused, seeking the best way to explain this plan. But Mrs van Weezelman's eyes were already clouding over, wandering back to the cello leaning against her knee.

'I want you to *play* to them,' he burst out. 'You've got to *tame* them. Weave your music around them, mesmerise them, make them sing, dance, forget all their murderous intentions!' His voice ended on a high thrilling note.

'Oh, music to soothe the savage breast! How delightful!' exclaimed Mrs van Weezelman.

'Bravo, indeed!' cheered his father, and played a cheerful jig.

'Yes, like that, but—' Wiggy struggled with his words, 'a little more *mournful*. I want to hear how water crashes over rocks, the way wind whips the sea into a foam, the wild loneliness of the black nights. I want to hear the gentle sucking of waves on shore…'

'Oh yes, *yes!* We will *create* the sea. We'll soften those cruel hearts!' And his mother struck a long forlorn note that hung like a sob in the air.

'And this!' cried Mr van Weezelman, plucking at his violin so that notes rose and fell like the cries of seagulls over waves.

'Yes, that's it!' Wiggy shouted. 'Now come quickly. Goodness knows what those monsters are doing right this minute!'

But Mr van Weezelman pointed his bow at Ludwig and shook his head. 'I couldn't possibly play in this state. Look at my shirt; it's stained and crumpled. What kind of an artist would I be to perform in this undignified state? No, I must go and prepare myself.'

'But there's no time!' shouted Wiggy.

'Hush, child,' said Mrs van Weezelman. 'Your father's quite right. We'll have to improvise you know, and that is a delicate matter. Now, go and run your bath, Herbert, there's a dear.'

Mr and Mrs Weezelman began to create while they waited for the bath to fill.

8 Tricked

The afternoon sunlight was fading from the Bolderack house, leaving a desolate chill. Boadicea sat near her grandfather, rubbing his numb legs from time to time, and waiting. There had been silence now for half an hour. She watched Tiger's eyes, fixed grimly on the Admiral. Shadows spiked his face, deepening the grey of his stubble, and the line between his brows. Nearby, G.C. Dan was fidgeting with his cutlass. He drew it out of its sheath, hawked and spat on it, and wiped it with his handkerchief. He did this five times, till he had no spit left. Then he hummed something grim and grisly under his breath.

Thick Mick, who'd been plucking at the hair on his toes, rolled onto his side on the sofa. 'What are we going to do then?' he said, yawning.

'Aye,' agreed G.C. Dan. 'I'm getting pretty sick of

twiddling me thumbs. Let's 'ave some action.'

Tiger took his eyes from the Admiral and said, 'You know we can't do nothing till our Captain arrives. He gives the orders.'

'Aye,' repeated Dan, whose vocabulary was not large. 'But he has to be called, like we were. That's 'ow the spell goes, don't it?' He stared at Admiral Bolderack, then Boadicea. 'Has to be named, like we were—by old Bolderack, or someone of his blood: someone connected with the swab 'oo banished us to that festerin' pit of an island.' And he glared at Boa, slitting his eyes to cracks.

'*I'll* never say that name!' shouted Boadicea. She was glad that she had never looked at the name of that fourth pirate—at least she'd had the sense to stop, then.

'We'll see about that, matey,' said Tiger over by the window. There was a nasty pause. Then Tiger spoke again in a lighter tone. 'In the meantime, why don't you fetch us some grub?'

'Now *that's* a good idea,' said G.C. Dan, and rubbed his hands together. 'What 'ave yer got in the larder for us? I fancy a nice bit of chicken, fried, with a few taties—*fresh* taties, with beans in butter and a dash of pepper. Aye, it'd make a nice change from fish and coconuts, coconuts and fish, eh Mick?'

'Aye Dan, that it would,' smirked Mick, and looked eagerly toward the kitchen.

'Well, I'll just go and see what we have, boys,' said Boadicea, and got to her feet. As she rose, the Admiral struggled against the ropes, and grunted at Boa.

'Couldn't you just loosen that rope a little?' pleaded Boa. 'It's far too tight—look, his ankles have gone all blue.'

'Poor Admiral Boldy-Woldy, is 'is little toes a-hurtin' then?' mimicked Tiger in a small high voice. Suddenly he bent down and pushed his face up against Admiral Bolderack's nose, and his voice grated like steel. 'But that's nothing, eh Admiral, to wot yer going to suffer later.' And he laughed with his mouth wide open, showing all the black wet gaps in his gums.

Boadicea went quickly into the kitchen. Admiral Bolderack had enraged her for years, but he was her own flesh and blood. He was a fussy, demanding, dreadful man, but she'd got used to him, and he had spent every night telling her wonderful stories. At the thought of that, she moaned out loud.

Well, all she could do right now was try to fix a flavoursome meal. Perhaps that would persuade them of her value as a live 'girlie' rather than a dead one.

She delved into the fridge, and reluctantly pulled out her secret hoard of fresh supplies. There was half a cooked chicken, two loaves of bread and an apple pie. She'd put a can of beans with it and some corn baked in butter.

While she waited for the chicken to heat through, she thought about Wiggy. What on earth could he be doing all this time? Even if he arrived with an army, though, somehow she didn't feel it would be enough. There was a power here—of old grudges, vengefulness. Yet she'd been hoping Wiggy would have come across some brilliant solution. She looked at her watch. No, perhaps this time his ideas, or his courage, had failed him.

'Dinner's ready!' she called, bringing the plates into the living room.

'Shiver me timbers, that's a smell to make the juices start in me mouth!' crowed Dan. 'Haven't had a whiff of food like that in years!' He clambered over to the table and sat down. Picking the chicken up with his fingers, he started to tear the flesh from the bone, shovelling it into his mouth in great handfuls so that skin and fat sprayed across the table and onto the floor. Thick Mick sat down happily beside him, with Tiger at the head.

Admiral Bolderack watched from his corner. His

eyes followed the scraps that went flying over the carpet, ground in well by six hairy feet. He moaned softly into his gag.

'Not hungry, eh Admiral?' said Tiger as he mashed up his beans. He scraped up the green mess with his fingers and stuffed it into his mouth, leaving it wide open as he swivelled the food round his gums. 'Couldn't we tempt yer with a nice bit o' chicken?' asked Tiger sweetly. Admiral Bolderack had grown pale and was making strange little whining sounds in his throat. He shook his head violently.

'Now we wouldn't want to be impolite. Mick, carry the Admiral over 'ere, and take off 'is gag. He's got to fill 'is belly like the rest of us.'

Thick Mick rose from the table. As he did so, Dan grabbed the last wing of chicken from his plate. 'You crookface, get away from my grub!' yelled Mick, but it was too late. The tender flesh had disappeared into the fathomless depths of G.C.'s stomach. His face was shiny with grease and contentment.

'Pig,' muttered Mick, cuffing him about the ears.

He stood over the Admiral. With one hand he picked up the helpless man by his collar and settled him down on a stool at the table. Then he untied the bandage around his mouth.

The Admiral had turned an awesome shade of

purple. With his gag off, his pent-up words exploded across the room.

'You bunch of ugly black-hearted curs!' he spluttered. 'You eat like dogs and behave like them too. I should have stuffed you into a kennel instead of an island, where you could have bitten each other's tails and scratched for fleas.' The Admiral's words began to tumble out like waves in a storm, so full of rage and trembling dignity was he. 'How dare you crash into my house like this, with your filthy ways, picking your toes on my carpet—hoodlums, scum you are, vermin let loose on the world. I'll not stand for your muck, slinging your swill around like a pack of hogs in a trough—'

Boadicea kicked his shin under the table.

'Glad to see yer've still got yer fightin' spirit,' said Tiger, smiling; but his voice was freezing. 'Feed the Admiral, Mick.' Admiral Bolderack pressed his lips tight. He refused to open them as a forkful of beans approached his mouth. Just then Boadicea switched on the light. The table and the three gruesome faces around it leapt into focus.

'Bless my mother, will you look at that,' exclaimed G.C. Dan. 'The only light I've seen in thirty years came up at dawn and went down at dusk. Makes a place real cosy that does.' And he leaned over across

Boadicea and switched it on and off ten or eleven times.

'Hey, you got one of them talking boxes, you know, what are they called—wirelesses?' asked Thick Mick.

'You mean the radio,' said Boadicea. 'Yes, of course we have. Over there.' She pointed to the radio sitting on the mantelpiece. Mick jumped up and fiddled with the dial. A woman's voice came on, speaking in Arabic. Thick Mick held it close to his ear and scratched his head.

'This lady's got a real bad cold. Can't understand a word she's saying.' But he continued to listen, hoping for a moment of illumination. Waiting was something he was used to by now.

Meanwhile, G.C. Dan was exploring the house with excitement. In the sink he found the garbage dispenser, which roared like an escaped lion when he turned it on. He jumped back in terror.

'Put your great paw in there, Dan,' called Admiral Bolderack, and laughed until he choked.

Dan spent the next few minutes stuffing anything he could find into its steel jaws. He watched, fascinated, as it chewed up chicken bones and serviettes with equal efficiency and cleared its throat for more. Thick Mick, in the meantime, had given up on

Arabic and had found the electric toothbrush.

'If you use the red one, you're a dead man!' roared Admiral Bolderack, and closed his eyes in horror at the thought of his new brush among Mick's black and broken teeth.

'Now *this* is what I call entertainment.' Tiger had discovered the television. He leant back in the Admiral's armchair, his legs sprawled out before him and he chuckled exultantly. 'Hey Mick, Dan, come and see this! Look at this little guy with the pipe and the muscles. He's plucky, even if he's a runt, I'll say that for 'im. An' a sailor like us, an' all!'

The two pirates scrambled toward the television. They pushed and shoved each other to get the better view.

'Strike me dumb!' cried Mick, and Boa giggled from the table. 'Look at that fellow fight. And he'd only come up to me waist.'

'Yeah,' said Tiger, 'but it's 'cause he's gobbling all that spinach, see? Every time he does that, his muscles get as hard as rocks.'

'Oh I see,' said Mick, nodding his head. But it was clear he didn't. Then he gave a great laugh and punched G.C. Dan on the arm. 'Cor, Dan, that big fat codger with the beard looks just like you!'

'Oh yeah? Well seems he's got a brain like a pea,

which is just about your size, Mick.' Dan was scowling, and he drew up his great legs, bending them at the knees so that Mick couldn't see.

'Give over, you two,' yelled Tiger. 'Can't hear a blessed thing. I like the way this little guy moves. He'd be handy to have on board, that's for sure.' Tiger watched every move of those flying fists, imitating them with his own. He punched at the air, left, right, left again, as if he were swatting a plague of flies.

When the credits came up with the song 'Popeye the Sailor Man', they all sang along with it, waving their arms in the air.

The men sat watching the screen for half an hour. They loved the ads with the pretty women showing off their legs as they drank martinis or baked cakes.

'Those females are even better than I remembered,' crowed Dan, slapping his thigh. 'Been away too long, I 'ave.'

Tiger was more surprised by the women train drivers, jockeys and lawyers. They wore overalls or sat at desks addressing important meetings. 'Will you look at that! Next thing we know there'll be women at sea.' He laughed nervously. Boa thought she'd better not mention that her Aunt Gertrude had been made captain only last year.

'That's a clever machine, that is,' said Dan, twisting

around to Boa. 'I've heard of them things before, but yer don't get to see them in my line of work.' He turned to Mick and said, 'They tell the weather, too, you know.'

Mick sucked in his cheeks in wonder. 'A pirate likes to know about the weather,' he explained to Boa.

Dan yawned and stretched, his belly popping out from his singlet like a surfacing whale. 'What's for pudding then?'

'Apple pie,' said Boadicea, and Dan let out a whoop. The pirates returned to the table, where the Admiral still sat, regarding the mess of smeared beans and coagulating gravy. As Tiger pulled out his chair, he spied a newspaper neatly folded on the mantelpiece, just as the Admiral had left it that morning.

'Ah, the daily paper,' said Tiger with satisfaction. 'I used to like a good read of the papers.'

'Have they got a Pugwash comic in that one?' asked Mick. He bounded over and leant on the back of Tiger's chair.

Tiger shrugged him off irritably. 'Don't know,' he said. 'What *I* like is the crossword.' He found the page, and extracting a greasy stump of pencil from behind a hairy ear, settled down to it.

'Hmmm,' he mumbled after a moment. 'Here's something we should know.' He looked over at Boa. 'Bet you can't answer this one. What's left when a wound heals? Four letters.'

'Scar,' Boa told him triumphantly.

Tiger grunted, printing it in. 'Well, wot's this then? It's round, and clocks and people have one. Four letters across.'

'Face.'

'You're right,' Tiger grumbled, surprised. 'Ah, here's one to stump you. Boy's name, rhymes with seat— four letters.'

'Pete!' Even as Boa shouted the answer, she was chilled by the look of sly triumph on Tiger's face.

'Gotcha,' he said quietly. 'You've just called up our Captain—Scarface Pete, me darlin'.'

Boa smacked her forehead in fury. Now her time was up. She could wait on Wiggy no longer.

She grabbed the packet of pepper and threw it in Tiger's eyes.

'Aarrrh! The brat's blinded me,' yelled Tiger, up-setting the table as he jumped up, and charging about in agony. As Dan reached for Boa, Tiger bumped heavily into him, and the two men fell headlong onto the floor. Boa made for the hallway, but Mick lunged after her. Quickly, she grabbed one of the upturned chairs and thrust it against Mick's stomach.

'Ooffah,' belched Mick and collapsed onto the floor. Her heart thudding, Boa hurtled down the hall and reached the door. She twisted the handle, but it was stuck fast. Oh, why hadn't the Admiral oiled the locks as he said he'd do? She kicked at the door, and heard the heavy thumping footsteps behind her. She gave a final twist to the handle, and it turned. With a cry she wrenched it open, and there, towering in the doorway, stood Scarface Pete.

9 Old Wounds

He was the biggest man Boa had ever seen. He must have been two and a half metres high, she reckoned, and his arms, folded across his chest, were as thick as tree stumps. Her eyes travelled down to his feet. One was bare and the other was a wooden point. She gasped, and suddenly felt herself being whooshed up into the air.

'So you're the Bolderack brat, eh?' said Scarface Pete. He held her up in the air, level with his face, as if she were a piece of dirty washing. She studied his face with awe. Not for nothing was he called Scarface Pete. A pink shiny line ran from his hairline, just missed his left eye, and ended in a bump at his chin. The scar stretched his eyelid, pulling it long and narrow, so that he had a permanent look of sizing something up. At the moment that something was Boadicea.

'Believe you called me,' he rasped. His voice was like stones rubbed together. 'I was beginning to think you'd forgotten me. And that would have been bad manners.' His breath was hot on her face. He smelt of bad fish and home-made rum.

'Glad you're here, Pete!' came a voice behind Boa.

'Yeah, good to see yer, old mate!' Dan and Mick rushed forward and clapped him on the back, trying to shake the hands that held Boadicea. He put her down with a thump.

'Aye, me hearties,' he said, 'it took a long time getting here. Thought I'd have to spend the rest of me days on that blessed island, counting me toes!'

'Aye,' replied Dan, 'the young cub was stubborn, she was, but we found a way round her, didn't we lads?'

'*I* did,' said Tiger, who had joined them. His face was streaming with tears, and he was blinking rapidly like someone with a bad tic. Scarface peered at him questioningly.

Tiger passed his hand over his face and muttered, 'Erh, just a bit of a, er, accident, like. Anyway, come in, Pete, and you can meet yer old friend.' He sniggered slyly at his captain.

As they trooped up the hall, Tiger gave Boa a

shove from behind. 'Perishing varmint,' he breathed into her ear. They entered the living room and Admiral Bolderack swung round to see the familiar face of Scarface Pete.

'Well, Admiral, it's been a long time,' said Scarface. He loomed over him, and cracked his knuckles. They made a sound like legs breaking. 'All trussed like a turkey ready for the oven, eh?'

'I never thought I'd see the day when wretches like you would set foot in my house,' the Admiral expostulated. 'Look at the state of the carpet, this table—you riff-raff, you disgusting, impetiginous brood of hogs—a pig would have more idea of how to—' Boadicea tugged hard at his sleeve. The Admiral fell silent, and stared at the floor.

'I wouldn't be worrying about the state of yer precious carpet, Admiral. I'd be worryin' about the state of yer *health*, if I was you,' snarled Scarface Pete. He leaned over and pulled at the rope around the Admiral's chest, squeezing it tighter. His face had darkened, and his left eye was almost shut.

Boadicea held her breath. Then Scarface chuckled and let go. 'Aye, always grumblin' on, you was, never a minute of blessed peace.' He settled himself in the Admiral's armchair, and pulled over another chair to rest his wooden leg.

'See this, tadpole?' Scarface turned to Boadicea and pointed at his scar. 'Got this during a battle, fighting beside yer grandfather. Jumped in front of a sword that was meant for 'im, I did, and I finished off the villain, too. No, if it 'adn't been for me, my sweet, you'd never of been here tasting the good life.' Scarface paused, and drew a finger down the length of his scar.

'But did I ever get thanks? Did he ever say to me, "Geez, thanks Pete, yer saved me life"? No. All I got was relief from night watch that one evening and all's-the-same, get-down-to-yer-work the next mornin'.'

'You did your duty, and that's what a sailor is required to do,' said Admiral Bolderack stiffly, shifting a little under his rope.

'Aye,' said Scarface Pete, 'and yer've no more got a human bone in yer body than this 'ere piece of timber,' and he tapped a tattoo on his wooden leg.

'Of course I was most grateful,' protested the Admiral, 'I realised the courage of your gesture. But you were a rowdy crew, and there'd already been a good deal of squabbling and squawking. Couldn't risk favouritism and the bad feeling that creates. I had the rest of the men to think of.'

The Admiral's eyes were shining as he relived the thrill of those dangers shared, and now he leaned forward eagerly.

'Do you remember that battle we had with the crew of the *Spanish Star*? Outnumbered we were by ten to one, but by golly, we gave it to them. Broke my sword, too, halfway through—'

'Oh aye, meanest bunch o' coots I'd ever seen,' chortled Scarface. 'Don't mind tellin' you I was wishing I'd stayed home with me ma when I saw 'em scrambling on board, yellin' fit to burst their breeches.'

'Yeah,' broke in Dan, 'they were all over the place like vermin, but I got me five and sent 'em splashing into the deep.'

But Scarface had stopped smiling. 'That was not the worst fight we seen,' he said quietly. Admiral Bolderack looked down at the floor.

'No,' Scarface continued, 'there was another fight that ended up very nasty indeed. Remember that one, Admiral? The last time we saw each other?'

'You and your motley lot there were the ones that started it,' the Admiral burst out. 'Coming at me like that in the middle of the night. I thanked God I'd always slept with my sword beside me.'

'No, it was *you* who started it,' said Scarface. 'You with your silly orders, and "ship-shape" ideas. "Feet on the floor, night watch!" or "Scrub that deck again, before I count to ten!"' Boa shivered as she heard

Scarface bellow those familiar commands in her grandfather's voice. The pirates were beginning to mumble and scowl around her.

'Yeah, and why was it always me that 'ad to go up the mast, when a storm was lashing and the waves were heavin'?' cried Dan. 'Nearly broke me neck a coupla times.'

'And what about the kitchen duties then?' said Mick, glaring at the Admiral. 'Me hands were gettin' wrinkled like old prunes.' Then his voice changed and he boomed, 'Scrub that pot again!' just as Boa had heard a thousand times, 'I want to see my face in it!'

'Aye, it was almost a relief to be on that island away from 'is ugly mug…at the beginning, that is,' Tiger added vengefully.

There was a pause, then Scarface spoke. His words were slow and careful, picking through the quiet like a rapier.

'But after thirty years, a man gets to thinkin' about all the things he's missing. He starts to get a little crazy. He can't wait to get his hands on the codger that sent him to this place at the end of the earth. 'E wants this codger to feel every bit of agony 'e's ever suffered—only twenty times worse. D'yer get my meanin', Admiral?'

Silence fell. It sank into the shadows, deep and leaden and sticky as quicksand. There was no way out now, Boa knew. No words, nor tricks, nor inventions could change the plans that Scarface had so lovingly prepared. Nothing stirred in the bowl of quiet, no one breathed, and cold certainty settled like the dark in Boa's heart.

Then suddenly, in a shock of sound, a long piercing note unfolded. It trembled in the air, gathering strength slowly like a wave rolling onto shore, and with a crashing crescendo, it broke over the room. Boa's heart thumped with shock. Then her skin began to tingle as she heard some high notes dance in, floating fragile as birdsong in the still room. Goose-bumps broke out on her arms, and she turned to look at the men.

They sat motionless in the throbbing room. Their mouths were open, as if to drink in the music, their eyes wide and glazed. They turned their heads toward the window, as the music shone in.

Now the melody quickened. Notes rose like questions, growing sweeter until their beauty became unbearable. Like living statues the men sat, scarcely breathing as the music twined around them.

'Open the other windows, be quick about it!' cried Scarface.

With a strangled yelp, Tiger sprang up. He ran to the window, pulled back the nets and flung open the sashes. In rushed the music in great rainbows of sound. And there, grouped together like a family portrait, were Wiggy and Mr and Mrs van Weezelman.

Boa stared. It was like waking up in the middle of a nightmare, and finding yourself in yet another dream. But there was Wiggy. He was conducting, his long skinny arms waving furiously in the air. His back was straight with importance, his head held high.

For just one moment Wiggy turned to look at Boa. His spectacles were hanging on the tip of his dear familiar nose. Boa waved and laughed and staggered as her knees sagged—she had no more control. Her body was suddenly light and she was content to let it go. Relief had flooded her muscles, and now she leaned back and let the music flow over her.

Tiger was shouting something out the window. As Wiggy raised his arms for the next song, he was yanked up into the air, sailing head first through the window and arriving, thump, on the living room floor. Then he was patted quickly on the head.

Tiger was not so rough with Mr and Mrs van Weezelman. 'Please come in!' he cried, and bowed very low. Mrs van Weezelman smiled politely and handed him her cello and bow. She hoisted up her long dark gown and climbed through the window. Her husband, shiny with his recent bath, followed her.

The men gathered around. They sat cross-legged on the floor, and Boa moved up to sit amongst them. Scarface Pete, his face glowing with excitement, brought a chair for Mrs van Weezelman to sit upon.

'What a grand town this is!' he exclaimed. 'Strolling musicians, and it's not even Christmas!'

When the van Weezelmans had arranged themselves comfortably, Wiggy raised his baton to begin the first bar. They swung into a hearty reel. It had a 'Hey-ho, and down we go, down into the deep blue sea' as a chorus, and the men knew it well. Their voices rang out, deep and surprisingly sweet, and Boa watched with amazement as they clapped their hands and drummed their feet on the floor. Soon she forgot to watch as the music lifted her up until she was floating above her fear, her voice mingling with the cries of the men.

10 Pirate Lullaby

Admiral Bolderack was undergoing a fierce struggle. He was staring disapprovingly at his crew, a sardonic eyebrow raised at the sight of their jerking knees and swaying torsos. But his left foot and then his right began to tap in time to the beat, and soon a note or two burst from his lips. A great shiver went through him, and he swayed back and forth under his ropes. Then, in a shudder of abandonment, he lifted his throat, releasing a long tuneful howl.

At the end of the reel, Tiger and Scarface slapped each other on the back.

'Bravo, bravo!' yelled Scarface, who had picked up the odd foreign word on his voyages. 'Encore! We want more!' And he leapt up to do a jig on the spot.

Considering his wooden leg and enormous height, Boa thought he was surprisingly agile. In fact, he seemed altogether different—younger, smoother,

looser. The harsh lines of his jaw had softened, and even the muscles in his arms looked more like soft pillows you could lay your head upon than the tree stumps they had seemed before. He beamed around the room but stopped at the Admiral.

'A bit more of this at sea, eh Bolderack, an' we'd all have been cheerier!'

Boadicea frowned and looked at Wiggy. His parents were tuning up and exchanging congratulatory comments about each other's performance. Wiggy called them to order with a wave of his baton.

The next song was an old sea shanty that sent the men into moans of ecstasy. One after another they leapt to their feet and circled in and out of each other's arms. Scarface Pete, jigging alone, used Boa's head as a maypole, and swung himself around her. Her hair got caught up between his fingers and it pulled, but she didn't complain as she know that a happy Scarface Pete was a definite improvement on an angry one.

Steer the boat ashore,
And a he-eave ho,
Haul in the billowed sail,
And a he-eave ho!

Now came their favourite—rounds. The pirates grouped themselves together, shoulder to shoulder, standing straight as flagpoles. Dan was first. Boa's eyes opened in astonishment. His voice flowed like water over valleys, rushing from high cliffs to warm shallows, rich and thick as honey. It made Boa think of faraway places, and colours hot like the sun. Tiger took the next round, and Scarface Pete blended his voice with theirs. Then booming out over the rest came the deep voice of Mick. His notes were so low they seemed to come from the soles of his hairy feet. He cupped his heart and his face grew red with emotion. The pirates sang together in perfect harmony.

As the song drew to a close, Mrs van Weezelman flung down her bow and burst into loud clapping. She ran over and kissed Mick on the cheek.

'A magnificent baritone! You have the voice of an angel!' Then she swept round to face Dan. 'And you, who taught you to sing like that? Such range,

84

such strength. You have an excellent tenor. Oh, what voices, what passion—I am quite overcome!' And she sank gracefully into the Admiral's chair.

The two pirates grew sweaty with embarrassment. They looked down at their toes. But their captain came to their rescue.

'It was you and yer partner's fiddling that inspired us, Mrs, Mrs—'

'Van Weezelman. But heavens, we have not been introduced. This is my husband, Mr van Weezelman, and my son, Ludwig.'

'Pleased to meet you all,' said Pete. Then he pointed a dirty finger at his crew. 'This 'ere's Thick Mick, then G.C. Dan, Tiger, and I'm known as Scarface Pete.'

Mrs van Weezelman stared, then stammered, 'What, er, original names. A definite, ah, musical ring to them.' Then she pointed at Admiral Bolderack, puffing under his ropes.

'And who is this poor uncomfortable man?'

'Well, this 'ere villain is apt to get a bit violent now and then. So we trussed him up just for safety's sake, like,' said Scarface Pete, looking a little uncomfortable himself.

'He doesn't look very fierce to me,' said Mrs van Weezelman. 'Why don't you untie him so that we can add another voice to our concert. He can't really give us his best with his chest all tied up like that. Most restricting, I'd say.'

Scarface Pete looked as if he were about to say something but Mrs van Weezelman turned back to her cello and settled her legs around its broad base.

Grinning, Wiggy motioned to his father, who was playing something by himself over in the corner. Soon, with bows and baton poised, they were ready to go on.

But Scarface Pete was having a difficult time over the matter of the rope. It didn't seem to have an end, having been tied with great skill, and years of experience, by Tiger. Scarface's fingers dug into Bolderack's flesh as he searched for the knot, and he didn't enjoy fumbling in front of his old enemy. The Admiral didn't help either, by gasping and heaving himself around, observing Scarface's efforts with a contemptuous eye. After ten minutes of struggling,

Tiger marched over and gave a quick flick to something under the admiral's arm. The rope unravelled and collapsed like a sick snake, and out bounced the Admiral.

'You never *were* much good at ropes, Pete,' he announced with a joyful whoop. 'You couldn't untie a ribbon on a present. I always told you: tie up your own prisoners, don't leave them to your crew. First-class practice in tying and knotting. But no, you wouldn't listen, and you never came to my lessons in slip knots, either.'

Scarface glared balefully at the Admiral. Boa watched the muscles in his arms grow hard again, and she could have kicked her grandfather.

'Let's not talk about knots and prisoners, Grandfather,' she said hurriedly. 'Why not just enjoy the music!'

'Aye, the girlie's right,' cried Dan and turned eagerly to the van Weezelmans.

They launched into 'Soft Nights, the Waves are Lapping'—a song so sweet it was known as the sailor's lullaby. The men sang in deep soulful voices, and near the end Boa saw tears glistening in Tiger's eyes. The Admiral stood with his crew, leading the refrain. He held the tune, steady and sweet. Scarface glanced at him, a strange smile twisting his lips.

When the song was finished, the men were puffing, and they settled themselves comfortably on the floor. Scarface Pete took the armchair, stretching out his wooden leg. The four pirates smiled around the room at each other.

'Aye,' sighed Scarface, 'There's nothing like a song to ease a man's heart. Must compliment the van Weezelmans—never heard music like it in all my days at sea.' And he exhaled deeply, his face smooth with contentment.

'You know,' he went on after a while, 'there's something to be said for a landlubber's life.' He scratched his jaw, his bad eye squinched to a slit as he concentrated on the business of thinking. 'I mean to say, 'ere we are, singing away like little birds, accompanied by the best fiddlers, sittin' in comfy armchairs that don't leak and 'aven't got 'oles in them.'

'Yeah,' broke in Dan, 'an' there's food in the pantry, *piles* of it. Wot'smore, it's all dry! There's a fridge to keep icecream in—'

'An' what about that codger on TV...Popeye. I could watch 'im all day,' said Tiger, looking at the television set wistfully. 'Not to mention the other great gadgets in this place,' he added.

There was a pause while the pirates pondered their situation. Boadicea sat still, hardly breathing.

She and Wiggy stared at each other until Wiggy's glasses fogged up and he had to wipe the lenses.

It was Scarface Pete who broke the silence. 'You know, lads,' he said softly, as if he were continuing his own thoughts, 'we're not so sturdy on our sea legs any more...nor so ready with our swords.'

'No,' agreed Mick, 'and I'm getting rheumatism with all that damp.'

'That's right,' said Scarface. 'I don't fancy a return to the clash and smash of them sea fights, neither. Lying at the bottom of the ocean with me lungs full of sea swill ain't my idea of a peaceful end. But listen, lads, 'ere's another idea.'

The tall pirate turned to Admiral Bolderack. 'What do you say, Boldy, to havin' a crew on deck again? 'Ere at your joint, I mean.'

The Admiral stared. Then he shuddered. He looked at Tiger, and saw the dirt gathering in black creases around his mouth. He looked at Mick and Dan, who smiled hopefully at him. Then he looked at Boa.

Admiral Bolderack was thinking fast. There didn't seem to be any other way out now, not as far as he could see. But just look at the filth of them! Still, anything seemed preferable to sitting on a desert island for the rest of eternity—or worse. No, looking at them now, he'd have to say they were a rough and savage lot, but perhaps, with a bit of cleaning up, they could be a crew again. After all, they'd be in his house under *his* orders. At the thought of that the colour came back into his cheeks. He glanced at Scarface Pete. Hmm, thought the Admiral, he was a big brute, but by Jove they'd seen some action together. Pete worked like a Trojan when he wanted to. The Admiral felt the old spiral of energy powering up his spine. By Gad, it *would* be good to have his men around him again!

'Well,' Admiral Bolderack's breath came out in a long thoughtful sigh. He stood up slowly, making them wait, and stretched the cramps out of his legs.

'Well,' he repeated, 'I guess it's all hands on deck and hoist the main sail!'

'Whoo-ee,' cheered the men and leapt to their feet. A great deal of back-slapping and nautical exclamations followed, until the Admiral called for quiet again.

'There are, however, a few conditions,' he said.

'Aye, and we've got some of our own!' replied Scarface, with a hint of a snarl in his voice.

But the Admiral went on. 'As you all know, I can't abide dirt and untidiness. Sloth and ill manners I will not tolerate—we'll be a team, and we'll all work fairly and equally.'

'Aye, that we will, with you doin' your fair share an' all,' said Tiger.

'And there's one difference you better get into yer head,' said Scarface. 'We ain't got no more sea battles to fight and storms to tame, so we can have our leisure hours, good and long. We're in our retirement now, well-earned I'd say, and that means feet up at night next to a cracklin' fire, and a bit of a sing-song before bed-time.'

'Aye, aye,' cried the pirates, seeing long evenings spreading before them, feet curled up warm as toast.

The Admiral cleared his throat. 'I never said I was averse to a bit of a sing-song. After a hefty day's work, that is.'

Boadicea ran over and hugged her grandfather. Then she grabbed Wiggy and kissed him on the tip of his nose. She was so excited she wanted to dance a hundred reels. With a new crew to look after, Admiral Bolderack wouldn't have time to organise every minute of her life. No, he'd be immersed in deep discussion with the pirates about all kinds of important naval matters. He'd chastise them, bellow at them, and old Scarface would bellow back. There'd be noise and arguments and jokes, and conversation at dinner. They'd sing at night and go to

bed late. No, even if those pirates behaved themselves, the household would never be the dull and
orderly place it had been.

Boa detached herself from the stunned Wiggy to
see the van Weezelmans packing up. Mrs van
Weezelman eased her cello into its case with the care
of a mother tucking in her baby.

'I think it's time we thanked the people who
brought us such happiness tonight!' Boadicea
shouted over the cacophony of gravelly voices.

''Ere, 'ere, the girlie's right!' chorused the pirates,
and the Admiral hurried forward.

'Indeed, by Jove, where are our manners!' he said.
'You'll have to excuse my men, they're a rough
bunch of sea dogs, not used to the gentle ways of so-
ciety.' His tone was apologetic, but his chest was all
puffed up with pride and satisfaction. He liked
saying 'my men'. It was almost as good as being back
at sea.

'It was our pleasure!' said Mrs van Weezelman,
smoothing her pearls over her breast. 'Such voices,
such harmonies!'

'Indeed,' agreed her husband, and strode forward
to shake the pirates' hands.

'But it was Wiggy who rescued—er, I mean—
thought up this wonderful treat for us,' Boadicea

interrupted. 'Remember Wiggy, Grandfather, the boy you've thrown out of our kitchen so many times?'

'Er, yes, good for you son, much obliged,' said the Admiral. 'I take it you'll be a fine musician like your parents when you grow up.'

'No, sir, I'm going to be a famous writer.'

'Well, there's nothing like a few sea stories to inspire the muse. Better get your pen out now, boy, there's plenty of material here.'

'So I see, sir,' said Wiggy, who had been making mental notes about exactly how many chins G.C. Dan possessed.

As the van Weezelmans trooped out the door (which was, after all, much more convenient than the window), Boa clutched Wiggy's hand. The smile she gave him made his nose burn. It was joyous and shining and generous, and at that moment, Wiggy knew exactly why he had liked Boadicea all this time.

11 An Attic for Two

It was one of those clear winter days, full of lemon sunshine and sharp shadows. Boadicea lay in bed under three blankets, and gazed out her window. Her book lay next to her, but she was too comfortable to move. Outside in the hallway someone was whistling. Boa looked at her watch and decided that she really ought to get up. Then she lay there just a bit longer.

The kitchen was empty when she arrived, but hot milk sat on the stove, beside a strong brew of coffee. She filled her cup and, taking a couple of pieces of toast with her, went to sit out on the deck.

The flag was rippling in the morning breeze. Admiral Bolderack, his arm raised in a solemn salute, stood between Scarface Pete and sleepy Tiger. When Scarface saw Boadicea he gave her a wink, and Boa rolled her eyes. She munched happily at her toast, and let her gaze drift over the morning. There was that fresh tang of dew in the air, and light daubs of sunlight buttered the hedges at the end of the garden.

Boa shivered pleasantly, and wrapped her dressing gown around her.

Later, when Boa came out on deck again dressed for school, the three men were still there. But they were no longer standing at attention. Scarface was leaning against the flagpole, saying something to the Admiral. Bolderack was nodding and pointing at the roof. Their heads were close together, and they were so deep in conversation that the Admiral didn't notice Boadicea until she had reached the gate.

'Oh, Boa!' he called, 'I won't be able to manage your lesson this afternoon, I'm sorry. Pete and Tiger and I are going to buy the wood for the attic.'

'That's OK. Don't give it another thought,' Boadicea yelled back, and swung her schoolbag over her shoulder. She waved at Tiger, who was watering the roses.

'They're comin' on a treat, don't you think?' he asked Boa, bending over a luxuriant bush. Boa stopped and examined them with him. The scent was strong as she buried her face in the velvety petals. She plucked one and put it behind Tiger's grubby ear.

As she strolled along the path she thought about Tiger's newly discovered passions, and chuckled. Roses, fresh coffee, and Miss Watson across the road —Boa had an idea that a good number of those roses would end up at No. 52 in the elegant vases of the Watson household.

'Hi, Wiggy,' called Boa as she drew up at his house. He started and dropped the book he had been immersed in. Boa bent down to pick it up. '*Four Doomed Men*,' she read, 'by Ludwig van Weezelman.'

'Hey, you've started the great book!' she said. 'When can I read it?'

'Soon, I hope, it's going quite well.' Wiggy was walking along with her at a great pace, describing the vast difficulties involved in writing a first novel. 'You need a lot of time,' he said, 'and experience. I'm only up to Chapter One, but I can see it all. I even know what's going to happen in the end. And that's important, all the famous writers say so. Dan's been giving me a lot of information about his battles at sea. I'm recording it all, word for word. Well, some of them I'll have to leave out of course.'

'So how's it going with Dan and Mick at your house?' asked Boadicea.

'It's great. Dan's taken over the cooking—you

know how he likes good food. He says food in packets is rubbish, and after tasting his cooking, I can believe it! Last night we had hamburgers with tomato sauce he'd made himself—it was delicious, kind of sweet and sour at the same time, and then we had chips. After that there was apricot pie with chocolate icecream. Even Mum noticed what she was eating. She said he's got the best tenor she's heard in years, and they're planning to do a concert with Dan and Mick as vocals. When she told them, they got all weepy and serious and looked at her like she was God or something.'

Boa stared at Wiggy. She'd never heard him put so many words together at the same time. His face was all hot and excited, and it seemed he still had a lot more to say.

'It's like living on a different planet, you know. Dan and Mick have got it all worked out that Dan cooks and Mick cleans. 'Course Mick thinks a land-lubber's kitchen is paradise after being on a ship, so he whips around with a dishcloth like it's a pleasure.'

Wiggy's face clouded for a moment. 'The only thing is they sing *all* the time. It's not that it's not tuneful or anything, it's just that they're singing different things at the same time. You should hear them, they go on all night. I don't know why the people

I live with never seem to need any sleep. Well, I suppose they don't have to write novels, either, or go to school at nine o'clock in the morning.'

Wiggy kicked gloomily at a stone as they passed into the schoolyard. But Boa's eyes were glistening.

'Maybe you'll get a bit of peace and quiet sooner than you think,' she said softly, and marched ahead of him.

'What do you mean?' Wiggy grabbed her shoulder and swung her round to face him. It suddenly struck her that Wiggy no longer seemed so skinny or fragile any more.

'The Admiral's been doing some thinking,' began Boadicea. 'With two extra men at our place, things have got a bit cramped. They've been bunking down on the living room floor, but they strew their dirty pants all around the place, and ash their cigars in the flower pots.'

'I know what you mean,' said Wiggy with feeling. 'We're lucky though because we've got a spare room, and Dan and Mick keep all their stuff in there.'

'That's just it. What we need is a spare room. So I said I'd give them mine—' she paused and smiled mysteriously, 'on the condition that we build an attic on the roof.'

She looked at Wiggy, who stared blankly back at her.

'A big attic,' she explained, 'as big as two rooms. It'll sit on top of Grandfather's room, stretching all the way over to the living room. It's to be made of wood, just like a ship's cabin. We can decorate it however we want—'

'*We?*' said Wiggy, his brows shooting up in puzzlement.

'Geez you're slow sometimes, van Weezelman. Yes, *we*. I'll put my bed in there, but there'll be stacks of room for us to both work in. You can call it your second room—your studio if you like—and you can come in the afternoons after school.'

Wiggy dropped his schoolbag and did a wild handspring across the playground. Sam Buzzby, who was coming the other way, just managed to miss Wiggy's two bony legs flying past his ear. He turned round to stare. So did the other children in the playground. Wiggy was not known for his great athletic feats at school.

'Van Weez has finally flipped his lid,' cried Sam. 'His friend Finkface probably drove him to it.' At this last piece of wit Sam ran around the playground with his demented monkey face, finally collapsing with laughter onto a bench.

But Wiggy and Boa didn't bother to reply. They were too busy making plans.

'So,' Boa was saying, 'I thought we could use that Persian tapestry thing your grandmother gave you, to hang like a partition between your space and mine.'

'Yes,' Wiggy said thoughtfully, 'I can't have any distractions, you know. Peace, quiet and concentration. I'll make a chest of drawers to keep all my papers in, and I'll bring my red mug to hold my pens.'

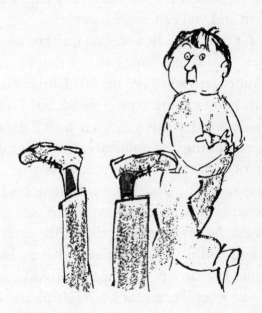

But Boadicea was thinking about colours. That tapestry was beautiful, woven in shades of deep crimson, purple and pink, stitched with tiny mirrors that glinted like the eyes of a thousand animals. It was so foreign, it would give a wonderful exotic touch to their room. And the Admiral had promised to give her those blue peacock feathers that he'd got on his last trip to Morocco. They'd be wonderful floating out of her cream vase on the mantelpiece.

'You can be my editor, Boa,' said Wiggy, breaking into her thoughts. 'I'll read you all my chapters as I finish them and you can make comments.'

'I'll be far too busy,' Boa replied quickly, horrified at the idea. 'I'm finally going to use that chemistry set that Aunt Gertrude gave me last Christmas. I've got a really good experiment in mind, but I haven't had a chance to try it out yet, what with flag-raising and deck-scrubbing and nautical lessons. But things are different now.' And she grinned at Wiggy.

Sam was sauntering back toward them, his hands in his pockets. 'Hey, Weezelman, you missed a great time by rushing off on that nature walk yesterday. Miss Gizzard invited this old man to visit us. He was once a cabin boy on a pirate ship. He told us stories about it—he even once met a famous pirate called Scarface Pete.' Sam smiled insincerely. 'What a pity